MW00748873

DINNER AT AUNTIE ROSE'S

Fourth Printing, August 1989

Design and graphic realization
Blair Kerrigan/Glyphics

Annick Press gratefully acknowledges the
contributions of The Canada Council and
The Ontario Arts Council

Canadian Cataloguing in Publication Data

Munsil, Janet.
    Dinner at Auntie Rose's

ISBN 0-920236-66-9 (bound). – ISBN 0-920236-63-4 (pbk.)

I. Ritchie, Scot. II. Title.

PS8576.U57D56 1984   jc813'.54   C84-098040-X
PZ7.M86Di 1984

Distributed in Canada and the USA by:
Firefly Books Ltd.
250 Sparks Avenue
Willowdale, Ontario, M2H 2S4

Printed and bound in Canada by
D.W. Friesen & Sons Ltd.

DINNER AT AUNTIE ROSE'S

Story by
Janet Munsil

Art by
Scot Ritchie

Annick Press Ltd.,
Toronto, Canada M2M 1H9

I hate going to dinner at Auntie Rose's house because my mom sets my hair in curlers and pulls them so tight that my eyes reach the top of my forehead. I have to wear my pink dress with the white sash. I hate my pink dress because the skirt sticks way out and I know my Uncle George will say, "Lucy, what pretty underwear you have on." I wish I had a rock to crawl under.

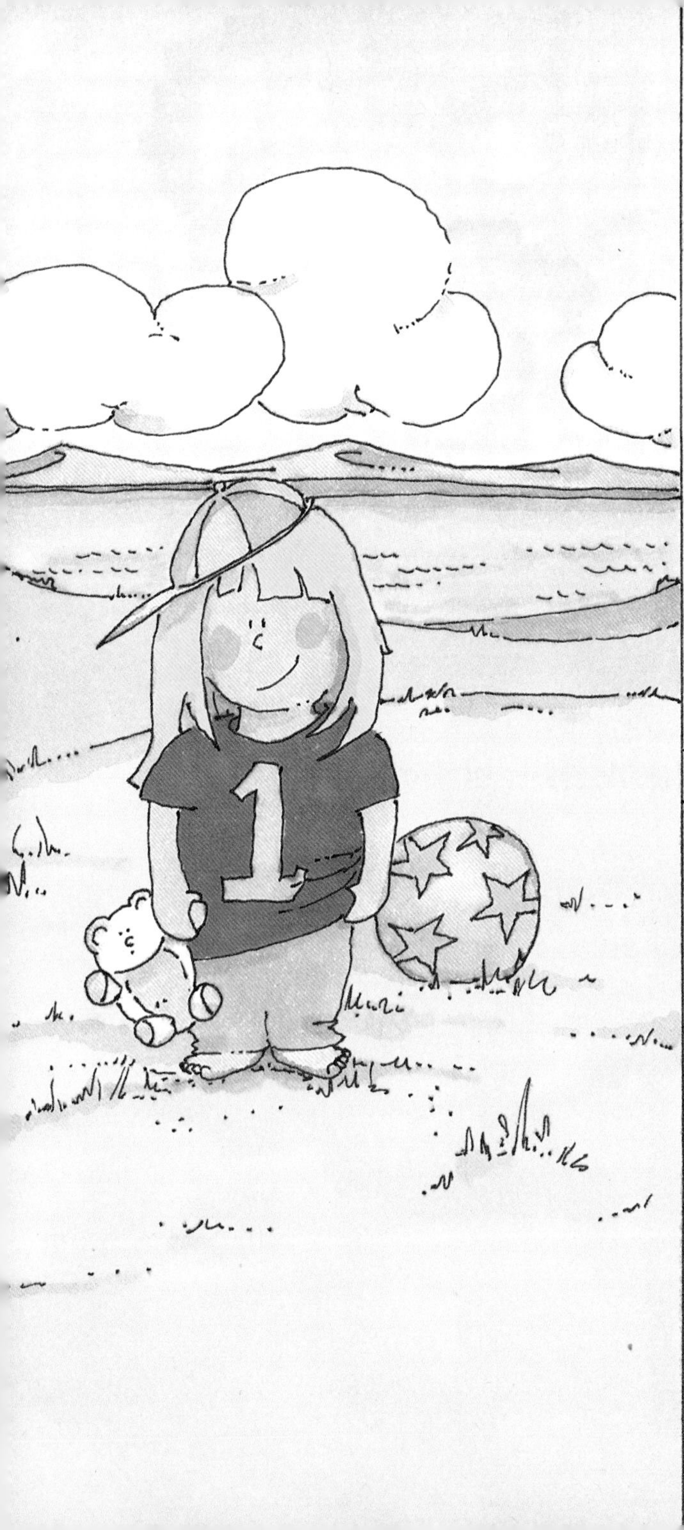
1
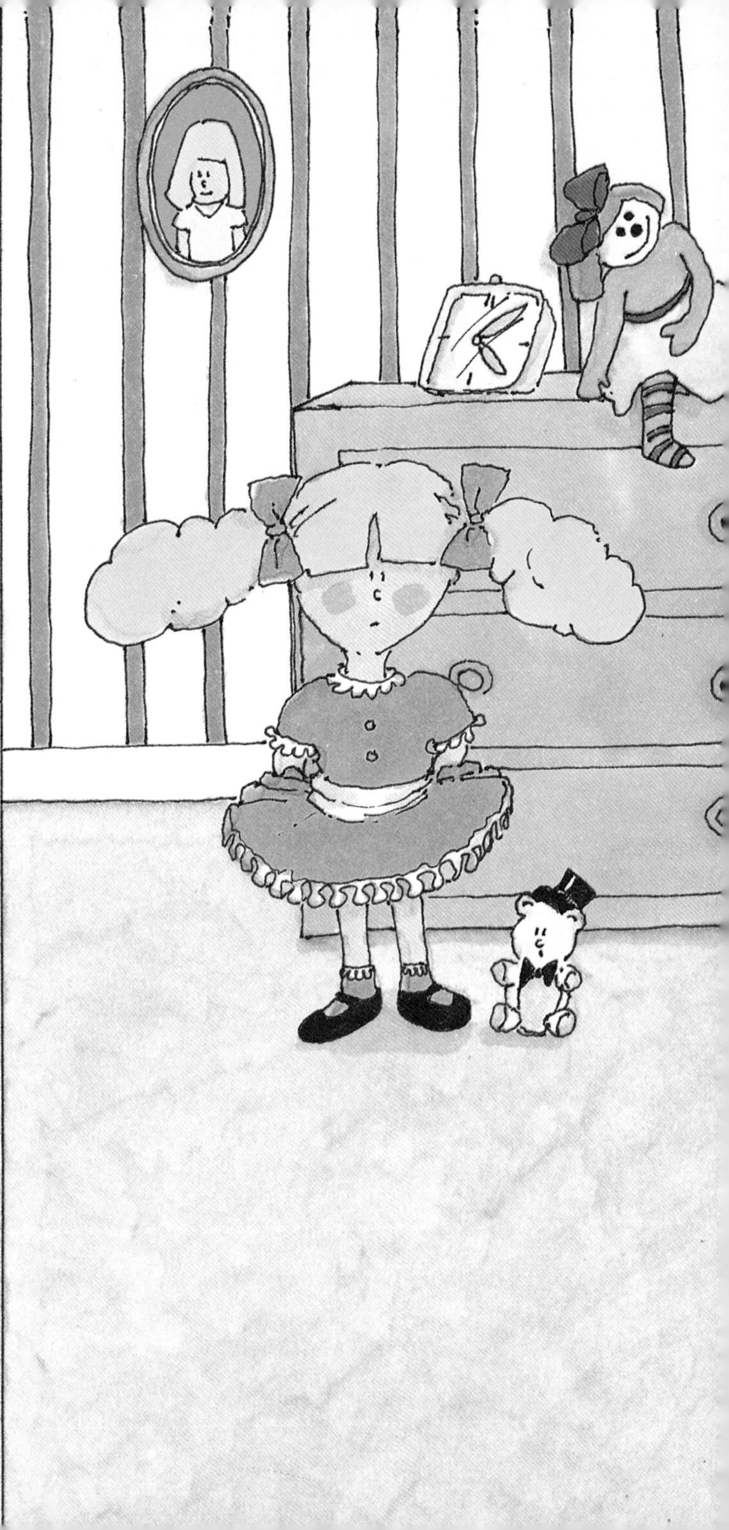

I hate going to dinner at Auntie Rose's house because before we even get out of the car, Mom reminds me to

stand up straight,

don't
shuffle
your
feet,

don't go into rooms
with closed doors,

don't talk with your mouth full,

don't pick
your nose,

say please and thank you,

AND
play nicely with Jeremy.

Jeremy is my cousin. HE IS A TURKEY.

When we get to the door, my mom straightens my sash and says, "Get that look off your face." I know that it's just my normal face, but I don't want to take any chances. I put on my, "Gee it's great to be here," face.

A sincere smile.

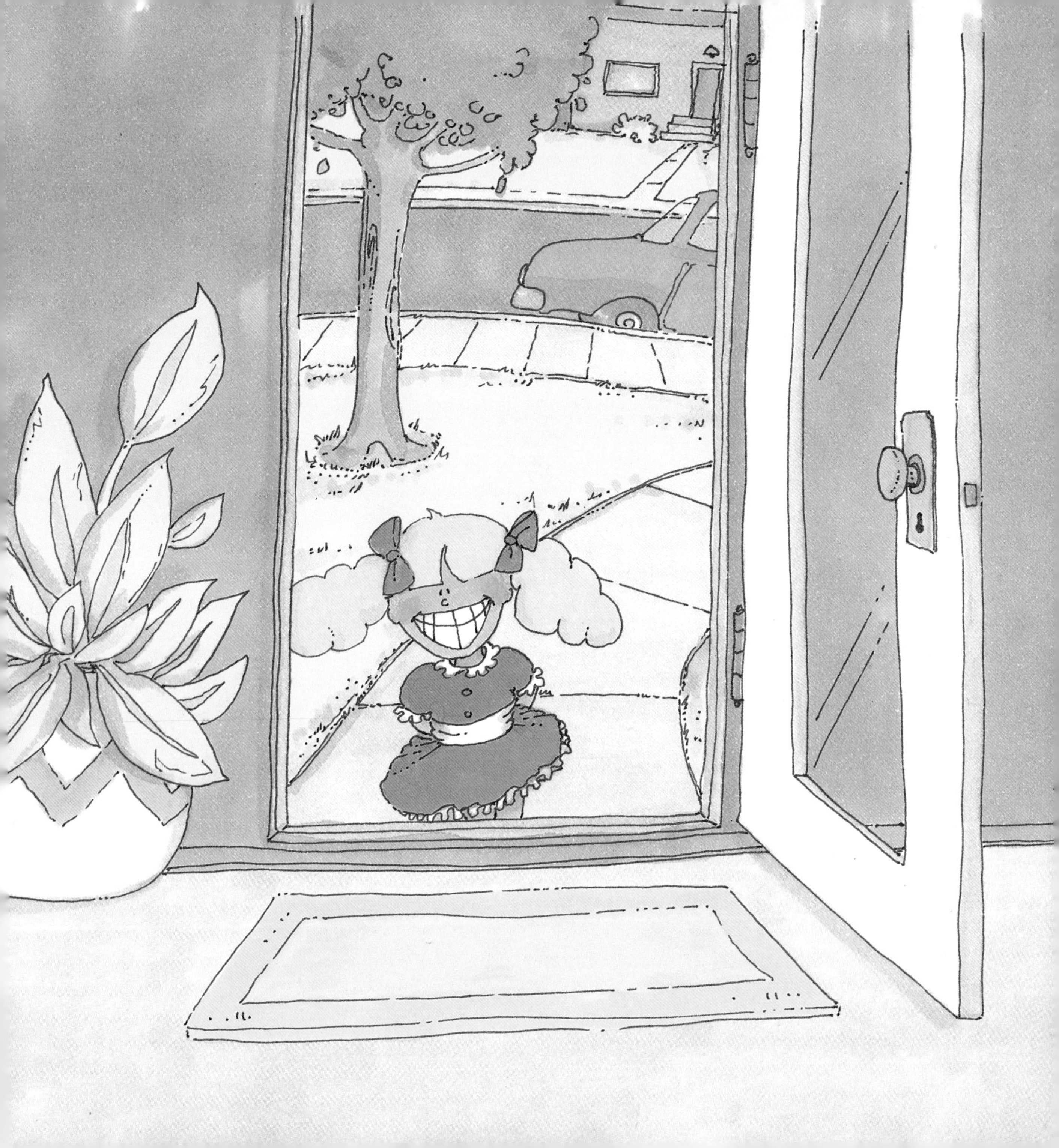

I hate going to dinner at Auntie Rose's house because she and Uncle George always say,

My, how she's grown!

She looks so pretty!

She looks so much like her mother!

She has the family nose!

It seems like only yesterday I used
to change her diapers!

They seem to think that talking about me is the same as
talking to me. It isn't.

Then Uncle George, who has a black mustache that looks like a cat's tail, asks me to sit on his lap, even though I'm six years old.

Uncle George smells like cigars. I hate sitting on his lap because he grabs my nose and says, "Look Lucy, I've got your nose in my hand." I know that it is just his thumb poking through his fingers, but I grab at it a few times. Uncle George has to be humoured.

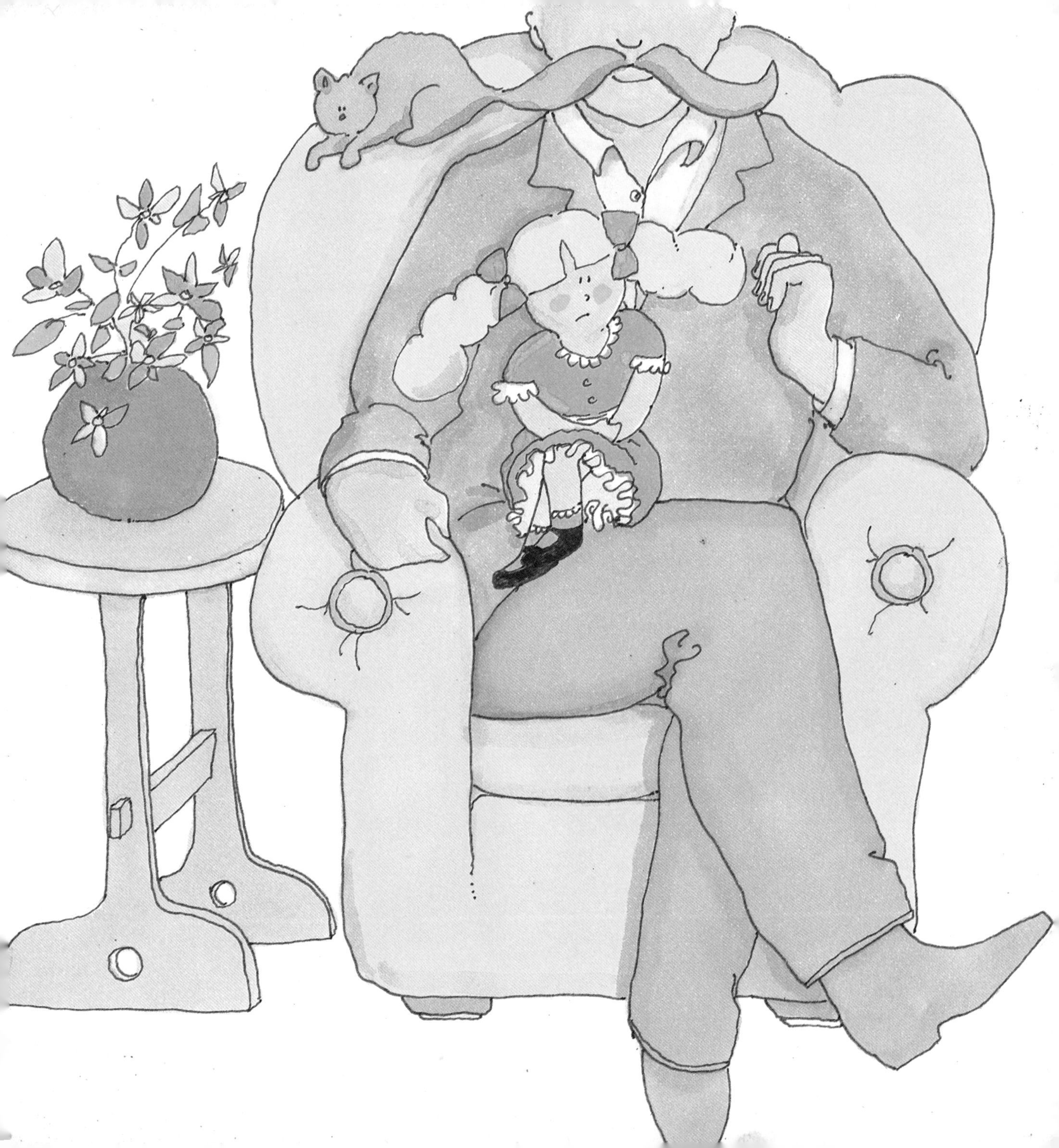

Mom says I should show Auntie Rose what I learned in ballet class. I ask if I have to and she says, "Yes, you do!"

I imagine that I am a great ballerina, dancing on the stage.

I do a deep curtsy when I'm finished, and Uncle George says, "Lucy, what pretty underwear you have on."

Sometimes Uncle George makes me want to scream.

Then Jeremy starts laughing. I don't know why he should laugh, because he doesn't even have to get dressed up.

I get mad and tell him to go jump in a lake and he says, "Make me." So my fist slips accidentally and his face gets in the way.

Mom says that's no way for a lady to behave.

I hate going to dinner at Auntie Rose's house because at the table Mom sits across from me. When I say that Auntie Rose should use "Dishwasher Sparkle" to prevent drops that spot, Mom says, "Lucy."

When she does that, I know I'm in trouble.

When Auntie Rose puts a huge scoop of pale green brussel sprouts on my plate, I try not to make faces, even if it smells bad and tastes worse.

Sometimes I forget to look like brussel sprouts are my favourite vegetable and Mom says, "Lucy, remember what I told you."

I remember.

I hate going to dinner at Auntie Rose's because Mom tells me to eat everything on my plate (even the brussel sprouts), because people are starving in Africa.

If there are people starving in Africa, I would be glad to send my brussel sprouts to them.

I try not to spill my milk,
but sometimes *it*

gets

in

the

way

of

my

arm.

I don't want
to talk with my mouth full,
but Auntie Rose asks me what I want
to be when I grow up and Mom says to speak
when I'm spoken to.

When Jeremy gets a bigger piece of cake than me, I don't want to call him a turkey, but I cannot tell a lie.

When I tap on the bottom of my glass to get the extra ice cubes out, I feel a kick under the table from my mom.

"Lucy..."

She forgot to remind me about that one.

I hate going to dinner at Auntie Rose's because after dinner we all go into the living room. I have to look charming and polite while the grown-ups talk about politics and sewing circles and inflation.

I'm not sure what inflation is but I think it has something to do with the price of corn flakes.

When I ask if it's time to go yet, Mom says, "Shhhh."

. . . and I know it isn't time.
Maybe not for hours.
Maybe never.

I hate going to dinner at Auntie Rose's house because when it's time to leave, I have to kiss everyone goodbye.

Auntie Rose picks me up by my ears. She leaves lipstick marks on my cheek that smear when I try to rub them off, and she wears perfume that smells like cockroach killer.

I don't like kissing Uncle George either, because his mustache tickles, and sometimes he has pieces of food stuck in his teeth.

I refuse to kiss Jeremy goodbye. I can't think of ANYTHING more disgusting.

I know that on the way home Mom will give me a lecture on my manners. Those are the worst kind of lectures, because you have to learn something from them, so that it doesn't happen next time.

How can I remember all those things for next time? I can't even count to two hundred yet.

At home, Mom combs my hair out and it really hurts because it gets all tangled from the curls. At least it looks almost normal again.

Mom hangs my dress up in the closet, because she didn't notice that it was dirty from the brussel sprouts I stuck under the sash, so I could flush them down the toilet.

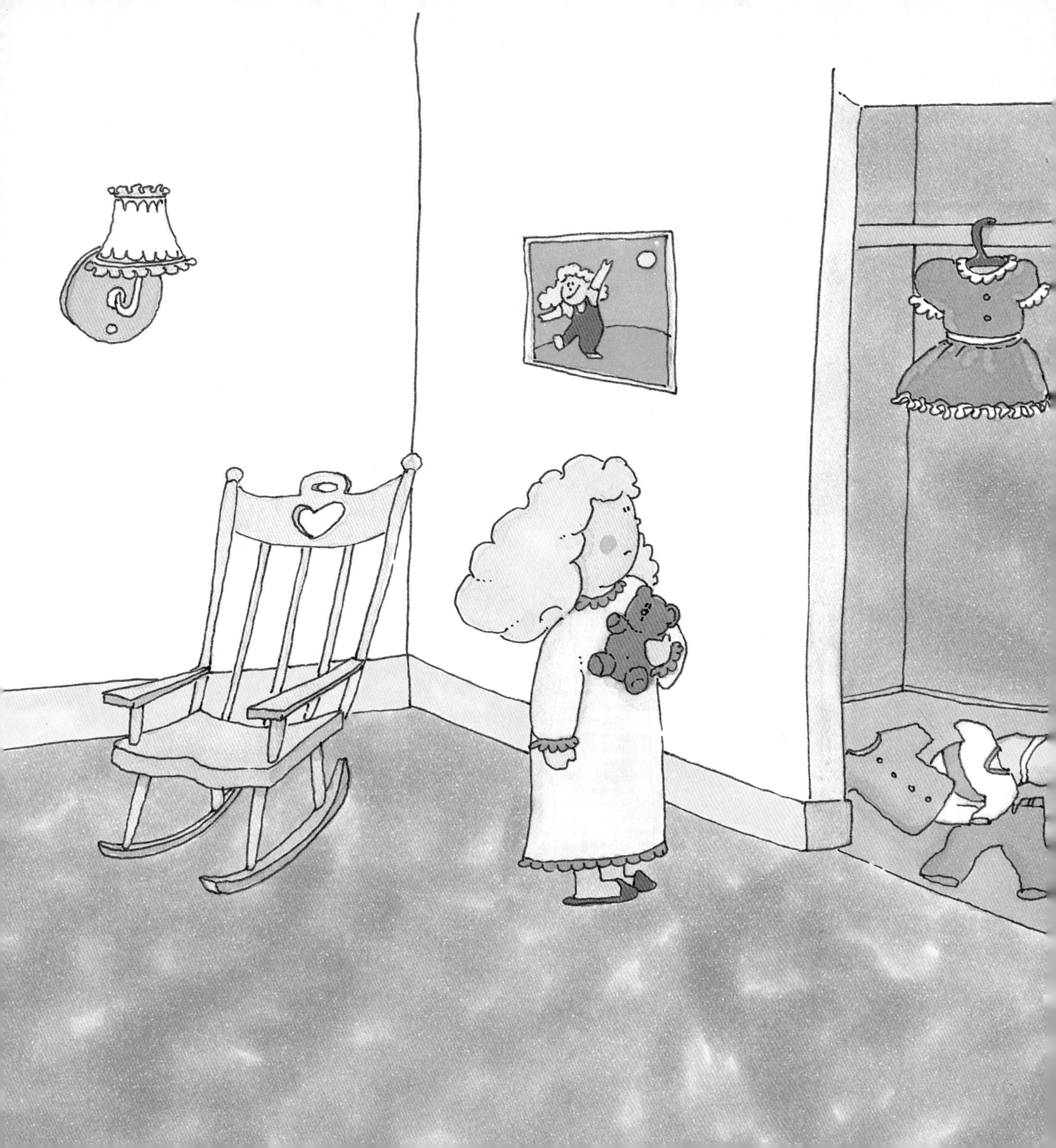

Then I have to go to bed, even though it's Saturday and I'm not even tired.

So, that's why I hate going to dinner at Auntie Rose's house.

But I love my family just the same.

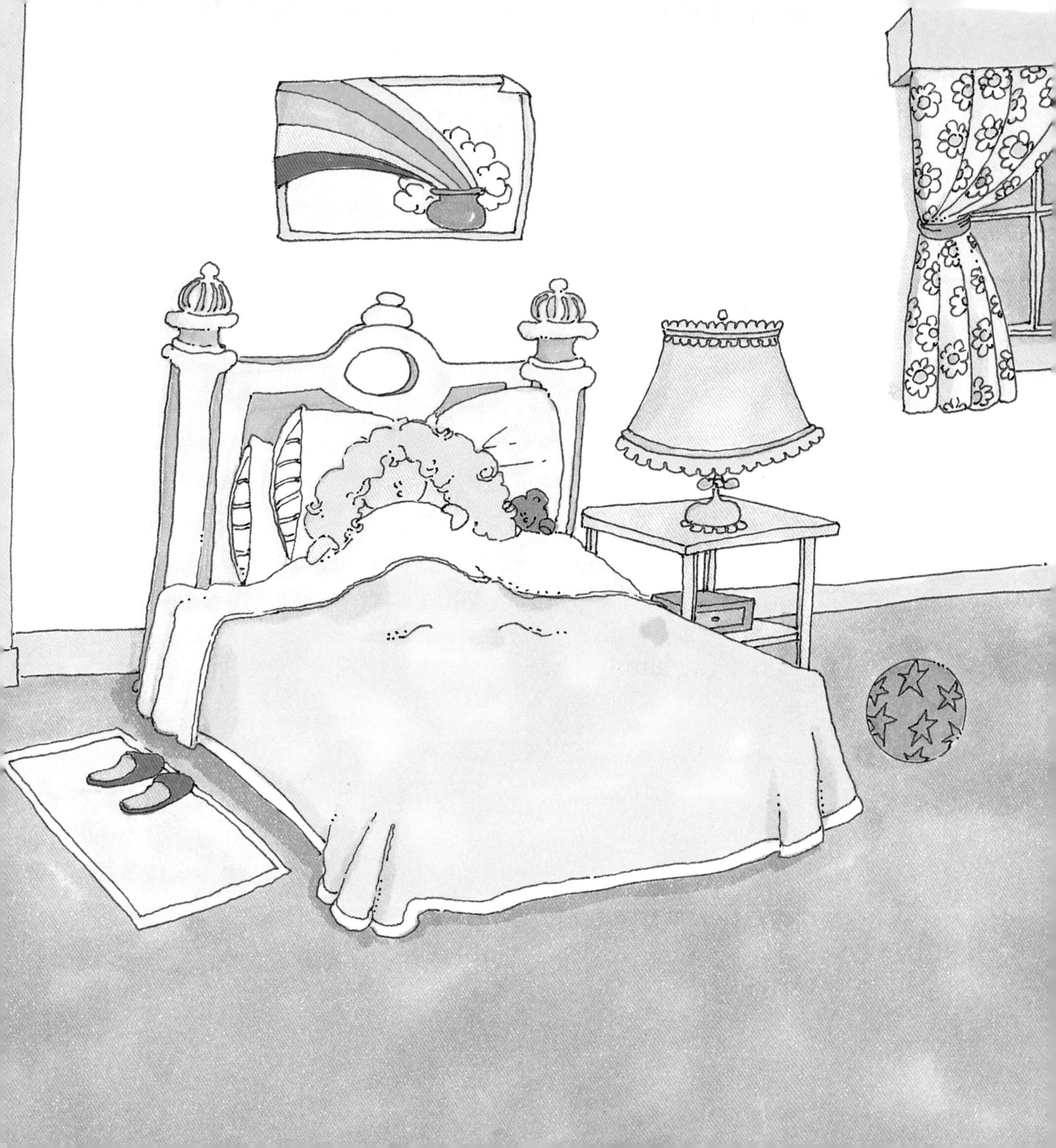